Silent Symphony

A Novel

By: Nyx Moon

WITCHES OF WORDS

Content Warning

Silent Symphony contains some themes and depictions that might be sensitive to certain readers. Please go to my website for a full list of content warnings.

ISBN: 979-8-9923898-1-4 (Paperback)
ISBN: 979-8-9923898-0-7 (eBook)

Any references to historical events, real people, or real places are used fictitiously. Names, characters, and places are products of the author's imagination.

Cover design by Witches of Words

Printed in the United States of America.

First printing edition 2025.

Witches of Words
www.witchesofwords.com

Contents

Prologue..4

Chapter 1 9

Chapter 2 13

Chapter 3 16

Chapter 4 20

Chapter 5 25

Chapter 6 32

Chapter 7 35

Chapter 8 41

Chapter 9 47

Chapter 10 53

Chapter 11 58

Chapter 12 65

Chapter 13 70

Chapter 14 74

Chapter 15 78

Prologue

The world was a symphony of sounds that night. Laughter, music, the clinking of glasses – all a celebration of my 5th birthday. Mama had gone all out, transforming our little apartment into a fairy princess wonderland, complete with twinkling lights and gauzy streamers that tickled my face as I ran through them. I twirled in my frilly pink dress, giggling uncontrollably as Papi dipped and spun me around the makeshift dance floor, our combined laughter echoing through the room, mingling with the lively music.

But Papi, always the doctor, always on call, got called away to the hospital. An emergency, he'd said, his face creased with apology as he knelt before me. He peppered my face with kisses, his scratchy mustache tickling my nose, and promised to be back soon, his voice a low rumble of reassurance. Mama squeezed my hand, her smile warm and bright like the candles on my cake, as we stepped out into the cool night air.

"Don't worry, mi amor," she'd said, her voice a soothing melody in the sudden quiet after the party's joyful noise. "We'll have our own little celebration, just you and me."

The city sounds faded as we walked, leaving just the gentle hum of distant cars and the rhythmic click of Mama's heels on the sidewalk. I skipped ahead, my pink dress swirling around me like a blooming flower, eager to continue the festivities with Mama. Then, a roar. Blinding headlights, like a monster's eyes, suddenly appeared out of the darkness, growing larger and larger with terrifying speed. Mama's hand tightened around mine, a gasp escaping her lips.

I remember trying to scream, to call out to Mama, but the sound wouldn't come. It was like a monster had its claws around my throat, squeezing the air from my lungs, stealing my voice.

And then... nothing.

Silence.

A cold, hard silence that pressed down on me, heavier than the weight of the world. I remember the rough pavement against my cheek, the sticky warmth spreading on my dress. Mama... Mama wasn't moving. Her hand, still clutching mine, was cold.

The world was a blur after that. Flashing lights, worried faces, their mouths moving but no sound reaching me. It was like watching a silent film, the actors' gestures exaggerated and meaningless. The silence that had gripped me in the moment of impact grew deeper with every passing moment. The symphony of my life had been shattered, leaving behind a void, an emptiness that would forever shape who I was.

I remember the smell of Mama's perfume, a sweet floral scent that clung to her clothes and lingered in the air, a comforting aroma that always enveloped me in a warm embrace. I remember the warmth of her hand in mine, the gentle squeeze that reassured me everything would be alright, no matter how scary the world seemed. I remember the sound of her laughter, a melody that filled our home with joy, a sound that could chase away any darkness.

But those memories were fading, replaced by the harsh reality of the present. The silence was deafening, a constant reminder of what I had lost, a cruel mockery of the vibrant world I once knew.

The world seemed dull and muted, devoid of the vibrant colors and sounds that had once filled my life, like a canvas painted in shades of gray.

I felt lost, adrift in a sea of silence, a lone ship tossed about by the waves of grief and confusion. The world moved on, the symphony of life continued, but I was frozen in time, trapped in the moment of impact, the moment the music died, the moment my world shattered into a million pieces.

The hospital was a cold, sterile place, filled with the hushed whispers of doctors and nurses, the beeping of machines, and the pungent smell of antiseptic. I sat in a small, white room, my pink dress replaced by a scratchy hospital gown, my body aching, my heart heavy.

Papi was there, his face etched with worry, his eyes red-rimmed and swollen. He held me close, his voice a low rumble of comfort, but his words were lost on me, muffled and distant, as if coming from another world.

I didn't cry. I couldn't. The tears seemed to have dried up, leaving me hollow and empty. I just sat there, staring at the white walls, my mind replaying the events of the night, the blinding headlights, the screeching tires, the suffocating silence that had stolen my voice.

Days turned into weeks, weeks into months. The world outside the hospital window changed with the seasons, leaves turning from green to gold to brown, then back to green again. But my world remained frozen in that moment of impact. The silence was my constant companion, a shadow that followed me wherever I went.

Doctors and therapists came and went, their faces a parade of concern and pity. They poked and prodded, shone lights in my eyes, and asked questions I couldn't answer. They spoke of trauma, of shock, of selective mutism. But none of their words could penetrate the wall of silence that had built up around me.

I learned to navigate this new world, this world without my voice. I learned to communicate with gestures, with nods and shakes of my head, with scribbled notes on scraps of paper. I learned to read lips, to decipher the silent conversations happening around me.

But the silence within me remained, a constant reminder of what I had lost, a barrier that separated me from the world, from the symphony of life that continued to play on without me.

I missed Mama's laughter, her songs, her stories. I missed the way she would twirl me around the kitchen, her voice a joyous melody, her laughter filling the air. I missed the way she would tuck me into bed at night, her soft voice whispering stories of faraway lands and magical creatures.

I missed the way she would hold me close, her warmth chasing away any fear, her love a shield against the darkness.

But Mama was gone, and the silence was all that remained. It was a silence that spoke volumes, a silence that echoed with the pain of loss, the weight of grief, the emptiness of a world without her voice, without mine.

I carried that silence with me, a constant companion, a reminder of the day the music died, the day my voice was stolen. It was a silence that shaped my world, my interactions, my very being. It was a silence that defined me, Maria, the silent girl, the girl who lived in a world without her voice.

Chapter 1

The sun beat down on El Centro de Oro, casting long shadows across the cracked pavement. A symphony of sounds filled the air: the rhythmic beat of salsa music drifting from a nearby bodega, the chatter of children playing in the street, and the distant hum of traffic. Unbeknownst to them, I, Maria Carmichael, a young woman with a quiet strength, navigated the bustling neighborhood, my world a silent ballet of signs and gestures.

I was a study in contrasts, my caramel-colored skin, a blend of my Hispanic and African American heritage, was often framed by the dark curtain of my unruly curly hair. My expressive honey-gold eyes, windows to a soul touched by both joy and sorrow, were often shielded from the world, as if guarding the depths of my emotions. Though my voice may be silent, my hands spoke volumes, their graceful movements conveying a depth of emotion that words often failed to capture. Each gesture was a brushstroke, painting vivid pictures in the air, my fingers dancing with a silent eloquence. Beneath my reserved exterior, forged in the fires of a childhood tragedy, lay a fierce loyalty and a deep capacity for love, waiting to be kindled by the right spark.

Since the hit-and-run accident that stole my voice at the tender age of five, I had learned to find beauty in silence. I revealed the subtle nuances of the world, the way sunlight danced on the leaves, the way a gentle breeze carried the scent of jasmine. But the world, with all its noise and chaos, could also be a lonely place.

My father, Isaiah Carmichael, was a man of contradictions. A skilled cardiothoracic surgeon, he spent his days mending the fragile hearts of strangers, yet he struggled to heal his own. The loss of my mother had left a void in him, one he tried to fill with his unwavering dedication to me. His love was a fortress, built to protect me from the world, but sometimes it felt like the walls were too high, too impenetrable. I knew he meant well, but his overprotectiveness often left me yearning for freedom, for the chance to navigate the world on my own terms.

Despite his stern demeanor, there were moments when his vulnerability shone through. Late at night, I would catch him staring at the photo of my mother that hung in our living room, his eyes filled with a sorrow he never voiced. In those moments, I saw the man behind the mask, the father who loved me fiercely but carried the weight of his own grief. It was in those quiet moments that I felt closest to him, even if we never spoke a word.

El Centro de Oro was more than just a neighborhood; it was a living, breathing entity. The murals that adorned the walls told stories of resilience and hope, of a community that refused to be forgotten. The scent of freshly baked pan dulce from the corner bakery mingled with the aroma of street tacos, creating a symphony of flavors that was uniquely ours. Yet, beneath the vibrant exterior, there was an undercurrent of change. Gentrification was creeping in, bringing with it sleek new townhouses and unfamiliar faces. The old and the new coexisted uneasily, the divide growing more apparent with each passing day.

Across the street, I often noticed a young man watching from his window. Ashwin Rivera, as I would later learn, had moved to El Centro de Oro only a few months ago, drawn by the neighborhood's vibrant culture and rich history. There was something different about the way he watched me – not with pity or curiosity, but with understanding. His dark, thoughtful eyes held a gentleness that made me wonder about his story.

In the evenings, I would see him practicing what looked like sign language in his window, his movements hesitant but determined. The sight stirred something in me – a mix of surprise and warmth. Here was someone willing to learn my language, to meet me in my silent world without presumption or demand.

My days were a routine of school, therapy, and quiet solitude. I lived in a modest apartment building, a relic of a bygone era, with peeling paint and creaky floorboards. The contrast between our aging building and the sleek new townhouses across the street was stark – a visible reminder of the neighborhood's transformation. Affluent families, drawn by the cultural richness of El Centro de Oro, were slowly changing the landscape, creating invisible lines between old and new, between tradition and progress.

I found solace in the small park at the heart of the neighborhood. It was a place where children played, their laughter ringing out like a melody, and where elders gathered to share stories of the past. For me, it was a sanctuary, a place where I could escape the noise of the world and find peace in the rustling of leaves and the chirping of birds. It was here that I felt most connected to my mother, as if her spirit lingered in the gentle breeze that caressed my face.

From my fire escape, I watched life unfold below. The elderly couple who ran the bodega, their movements synchronized after decades together. The group of children who played hopscotch on the sidewalk, their games punctuated by laughter and shouts. And now this mysterious young man, whose presence across the street added a new dimension to my daily observations.

I wondered about him; about the life he lived beyond those gleaming windows. Was he a dreamer, a kindred spirit who understood the quiet beauty of solitude? Or was he simply curious about the silent girl with the soulful eyes? Perhaps, in time, our paths would cross, and I would learn his story. But for now, he remained a mystery, a silent observer from a world apart, yet somehow bridging the gap between our separate silences.

Chapter 2

The year I turned eighteen, a whirlwind of a girl named Jewel McMillan moved in next door. Jewel, with her naturally curly blonde hair—perhaps inherited from her pale-skinned father—and sparkling green eyes that shone with mischief, was a breath of fresh air, especially since I mostly kept to myself. Her infectious laughter was a stark contrast to the quiet solitude I'd become accustomed to. With her bright eyes and inquisitive spirit, she'd come knocking almost every day, eager to share her latest adventure or show off a new drawing. It became our routine, a burst of sunshine in the quiet rhythm of my days that I began to crave.

• • •

Her parents, Ashley and Ted McMillan, were a different story. Ashley, with her haunted brown eyes and nervous laughter, seemed to carry the weight of the world on her slender shoulders. Ted, on the other hand, was a man of few words, his presence radiating a quiet intensity that bordered on intimidating. Jewel, with her blonde curls and mischievous green eyes, seemed a world apart from both of them.

Jewel was a chatterbox, her words tumbling over each other in her eagerness to share everything and nothing. I, in contrast, was a listener, my world a silent symphony of gestures and expressions. Yet, despite our differences, we found a rhythm, a way to connect across the divide of our contrasting worlds.

She would sit beside me, her small hand resting on my arm as she chattered about her day, her dreams, her fears. I would watch her lips move, my fingers itching to translate her words into the graceful dance of sign language. Sometimes, I would catch a word or two, enough to piece together the gist of her stories. Other times, I would simply bask in the warmth of her presence, the sound of her voice a soothing melody in the quiet of my world. I'd often find myself tracing the shape of her curls with my eyes, marveling at their golden hue, so unlike her mother's darker hair. Or I'd get lost in the depths of her sparkling green eyes, eyes that held a mischievous glint and a wisdom beyond her years.

One day, as she was recounting her latest adventure in the playground, she paused, her brow furrowed in thought. "Maria," she began, her voice soft and curious, "Can you teach me to talk with my hands?"

My heart skipped a beat. It was a question I hadn't expected, a request that opened a door to a whole new level of connection. I smiled, grabbing my notepad to write, "Yes, Bunny, I can teach you."

Her face lit up, her eyes sparkling with excitement. "Really?" she asked, her voice filled

● ● ●

with wonder.

I nodded, my smile widening. "Really," I confirmed, scribbling the word quickly on the pad.

From that day on, our routine took on a new dimension. We would sit together, my hands guiding her as I taught her the alphabet, the basic signs, the rhythm and flow of sign language. She was a quick learner, her fingers mimicking mine with surprising dexterity. Her laughter filled the air as she stumbled over new signs, her enthusiasm infectious.

I found myself looking forward to our

lessons, to the way her face lit up when she grasped a new sign, to the way her fingers danced with newfound fluency. It was a joy to share my world with her, to watch her embrace the language that had once been my only solace.

As the days turned into weeks, our bond deepened, our connection strengthened by the shared language of our hands. It was a language of laughter, of friendship, of love. It was a language that transcended the barriers of our contrasting worlds, uniting us in a symphony of silence and sound.

Chapter 3

The fire escape was my sanctuary, a small haven away from the watchful eyes of my father. It was here, perched above the bustling streets of El Centro de Oro, that I felt most at peace, most myself. I was sitting on the fire escape, writing in my diary. When I have time I write songs. I know I will never get to sing them, but it makes me feel closer to my mom.

I closed my eyes, the melody of a new song playing out in my mind. It was a song about loss, about longing, about the silence that had become my constant companion. But it was also a song about hope, about resilience, about the strength I had found in the quiet spaces of my world.

As I scribbled the lyrics into my diary, I felt a familiar gaze upon me. I glanced up, startled by a feeling of being watched, and met the gaze of the mystery man across the street. His dark, mysterious eyes held a strange fixation, locking onto mine with an almost unsettling focus. It was as if he could see right through me, past my carefully constructed walls, into the depths of my soul.

I couldn't help but wonder about him, about the thoughts swirling behind those enigmatic eyes. Was he simply curious about the silent girl who spent her evenings scribbling in a diary? Or did he see something more, something deeper, in the

• • •

depths of my soul?

I met his gaze for a fleeting moment, a silent acknowledgment passing between us. Then, I lowered my eyes, my cheeks flushing with a warmth that had nothing to do with the summer heat.

The melody of my song played on, a bittersweet symphony of emotions echoing in the silence of my heart.

And as I sat there, bathed in the warm glow of the setting sun, I couldn't help but feel a glimmer of anticipation, a sense that something new, something exciting, was about to unfold. The

• • •

mystery man across the street was a puzzle, an

enigma, a potential disruption to the quiet rhythm of

my life. And for the first time in a long time, I

found myself craving the unknown, the unexpected,

the possibility of a connection that could break

through the silence and awaken my heart.

Perhaps it was the yearning in his eyes, or

maybe it was the way he seemed to see beyond my

silence, to the heart of who I was. Whatever it was,

it sparked a flicker of curiosity within me, a desire

to know more about this enigmatic stranger.

I closed my diary, tucking it safely away,

and turned my attention back to the mystery man.

• • •

He was still watching me, his gaze unwavering. I couldn't help but smile, a warmth spreading through me despite my usual reserve.

In that moment, I felt a connection, a silent spark that transcended the distance between us. It was a feeling I hadn't experienced in a long time, a feeling that whispered of possibilities, of hope, of a future that could be filled with more than just silence.

His gaze was a lifeline, a beacon of warmth in the sometimes-isolating quiet of my world. It was a connection that went beyond words, a shared understanding that resonated deep within my soul.

I found myself drawn to his steady presence, to the way he seemed to see me, truly see me, beneath the layers of silence and reserve. It was a feeling I had almost forgotten, a feeling of being understood, of being acknowledged, of being seen.

In the quiet solitude of my world, I had become accustomed to being an observer, a spectator in the symphony of life. But his gaze, his unwavering attention, sparked a longing within me, a desire to step out of the shadows and into the light.

It was a yearning for connection, for companionship, for a shared experience that could transcend the barriers of my silent world. It was a hope that perhaps, just perhaps, this stranger across the street could be the one to break through the silence and awaken my heart to the symphony of life.

But as I basked in the warmth of his attention, a flicker of fear danced in the shadows of my heart. The memories of schoolyard taunts and whispered insults echoed in the silence of my mind. Would he, too, see me as different, as flawed, as less than whole?

I hesitated, fear gripping my heart. Was it worth the risk? The potential for connection, for understanding, was a siren song, luring me towards the rocky shores of vulnerability. But what if it was all an illusion? What if, like the fleeting echoes of laughter in a silent world, it vanished as quickly as it appeared, leaving me stranded in a sea of disappointment and renewed heartache?

The memories of schoolyard taunts and whispered insults were a chorus of warnings, reminding me of the pain that came with opening myself up to a world that didn't understand. Was I strong enough to weather another storm of rejection? Did I dare to hope that this time could be different?

The silent spark flickered, a fragile flame in the face of my doubt. It was a chance, a possibility, a whisper of a future where I could be seen not for my silence, but for the symphony of emotions that played within my heart. But was I brave enough to reach for it, knowing the potential cost?

My smile faded; the warmth replaced by a chill that seeped into my bones. I stood up abruptly, the metal of the fire escape cold beneath my bare feet. Without a backward glance, I retreated back into the sanctuary of my apartment, the questions lingering like ghosts in the quiet space of my mind.

Chapter 4

The sterile halls of UCLA Medical Center stretched before us, their pristine white walls reflecting the afternoon California sun. The Voice Center for Medicine and the Arts occupied an entire wing of the hospital, its modern architecture a testament to the cutting-edge procedures performed within. My footsteps echoed alongside Papi's as we followed the receptionist to Dr. Gerald Berke's office, my heart pounding with each step.

The office itself was a study in contrasts - warm wooden furniture against stark medical equipment, detailed anatomical models of the human larynx displayed alongside framed achievements. Dr. Berke, a distinguished figure with silver-streaked hair and kind eyes, rose to greet us.

"Maria, Dr. Carmichael, welcome," he said, gesturing to the comfortable chairs facing his desk. "I've been reviewing Maria's case extensively."

He pulled up detailed imaging of my vocal cords on his computer screen, the damage from the childhood accident clearly visible even to my untrained eyes. Using a laser pointer, he indicated the scarred areas that had robbed me of my voice.

"The procedure we're proposing is revolutionary," Dr. Berke explained, his enthusiasm evident as he pulled up diagrams of the surgical approach. "We've developed a technique that combines stem cell therapy with microsurgical reconstruction. First, we harvest stem cells from Maria's own tissue to grow new vocal cord material in the lab. This reduces the risk of rejection significantly."

I watched my father's face, noting how his medical training made his expression more focused as he absorbed the technical details. As a cardiothoracic surgeon, he understood the complexities better than most parents would.

"The actual surgery involves a series of delicate steps," Dr. Berke continued, showing us a computer simulation. "We make a small incision in the neck to access the larynx. Using microsurgical techniques, we carefully remove the scarred tissue while preserving the surrounding healthy structures. Then we implant the lab-grown tissue, using a revolutionary scaffolding technique to ensure proper alignment and function."

The animation showed the intricate procedure in detail - the careful separation of tissues, the precise placement of the new vocal cord material, the delicate suturing that would hold everything in place while it healed.

"Recovery would involve several weeks of complete vocal rest, followed by intensive voice therapy," he explained. "The process is lengthy, but with dedication and proper rehabilitation, there's a strong possibility Maria could regain significant vocal function."

"Maria is an excellent candidate," Dr. Berke said, his eyes kind as he looked between my father and me. "Her initial trauma was clean, and her young age works in her favor. The stem cells from younger patients typically show better growth and integration patterns."

I watched my father's face carefully. His expression remained neutral, but I could see the tension in his jaw, the way his hands fidgeted in his lap. As a doctor himself, he understood both the potential and the risks all too well.

• • •

"However," Dr. Berke continued, his tone growing more serious, "I must be clear about the risks. While our success rate is promising, this is still an experimental procedure. There's a small but significant risk of complications, including..." he paused, choosing his words carefully, "in extremely rare cases, death."

He went on to detail the specific risks: infection, bleeding, adverse reaction to anesthesia, damage to surrounding structures, and the possibility that the procedure might not work at all. Each potential complication was like a weight being added to my father's shoulders.

• • •

My father's face drained of color as he turned to me, his eyes filled with a fear I hadn't seen since the accident that took my mother. The memory of that night hung between us - the screeching tires, the shattering glass, the silence that followed.

"Absolutely not," he said firmly. "I won't risk losing you too." His voice cracked with emotion.

I started to protest, but he cut me off with a sharp gesture. The fear in his eyes was raw, primal - the fear of a father who had already lost too much.

"No, Maria. I said no. We'll find another

way."

Dr. Berke watched our exchange with understanding in his eyes. He'd likely seen similar scenes play out in his office before - the battle between hope and fear, between possibility and risk.

I turned to Dr. Berke. "Can I have time to think about it?"

The doctor nodded sympathetically. "Of course. This isn't a decision to be made lightly. Take all the time you need. The procedure isn't going anywhere, and we want you to be completely comfortable with your choice."

He handed us a thick folder containing detailed information about the surgery, recovery process, and statistical outcomes from their preliminary trials. "Review these materials. Discuss it as a family. If you have any questions, my office is always available."

As we left the medical center, the California sun felt less warm somehow. The weight of the decision pressed down on us, heavier than the folder in my hands. My father remained silent during our drive to the airport, his knuckles white against the steering wheel. I knew this wasn't the end of the discussion, but for now, the silence between us spoke volumes.

Looking out the window at the passing landscape, I thought about voices - my mother's, lost forever in the crash; my own, trapped behind scarred vocal cords; my father's, tight with fear at the prospect of losing me too. The possibility of speaking again beckoned like a distant star, beautiful but perhaps too dangerous to reach.

The folder sat heavy in my lap, filled with promises and warnings, hope and fear. Inside were detailed diagrams of what the surgery could do, statistics about success rates, and testimonials from patients who had undergone similar procedures. But numbers and medical terms couldn't capture the real weight of this decision - the choice between accepting my silence and risking everything for a chance to break it.

As the airport came into view, I realized that this journey was about more than just regaining my voice. It was about facing fears, about the price of hope, about the complicated love between a father and daughter. Whatever decision we ultimately made would change us both forever.

For now, though, we existed in this moment of uncertainty, suspended between what was and what could be, our silence filled with all the words we couldn't - or wouldn't - say.

• • •

Chapter 5

The worn, concrete steps leading up to our apartment building were my other sanctuary, a place where I could escape the confines of my silent world and connect with the rhythm of the city. Where Jewel and I would meet up for our chats. The sun had just dipped below the horizon, casting long shadows that danced across the cracked pavement. I sat with my back against the cool stone, my diary open in my lap, the pen a familiar extension of my hand.

The words flowed onto the page, a torrent of emotions and thoughts that had been swirling within me since our visit to UCLA. The hope, the fear, the uncertainty – it all poured out, a silent symphony of words that only my diary could hear.

"Dear Diary," I wrote, my pen scratching against the paper, "Today, I met with Dr. Berke. She spoke of miracles, of possibilities, of a future where my voice could be heard again. But she also spoke of risks, of complications, of the ever-present shadow of death."

I paused, my hand hovering over the page, the weight of the decision pressing down on me. Was I brave enough to face the unknown, to embrace the risk, to fight for a voice that might forever remain silent?

"Papi is scared," I continued, my pen

resuming its dance across the page. "He's afraid of losing me, of the surgery stealing the daughter he has left. I understand his fear, but I can't let it dictate my life. I need to speak. I need to be heard."

A shadow fell across my page, and I looked up to see Jewel standing before me, her bright eyes shining with curiosity.

"Whatcha writing, Maria?" she asked, her voice a cheerful melody that broke through my thoughts.

"It's a secret," I signed, a playful smile curving my lips.

Jewel giggled, her pigtails bouncing. "Tell me!" she pleaded, her hands signing the words with surprising fluency.

I was amazed by how quickly she had picked up sign language. She was natural, her fingers mimicking my movements with effortless grace. It was a joy to watch her embrace this new form of communication, to see her connect with my silent world.

"Okay, okay," I signed, relenting. "I'm writing about my trip to the doctor. They might be able to give me my voice back."

Jewel's eyes widened in surprise. "Really?" she signed, her excitement palpable. "That's amazing!"

I nodded, a warmth spreading through me at her enthusiasm. "But it's a risky surgery," I added, my fingers slowing, the fear creeping back in.

Jewel's face fell. "Risky?" she signed, her brow furrowed with concern.

"Yes," I confirmed. "There's a chance it might not work. Or worse..."

I trailed off, unable to sign the word "death." The thought of it, of losing this chance, of leaving

Papi alone, was too much to bear.

Jewel, sensing my distress, reached out and took my hand, her small fingers squeezing mine in a gesture of comfort. "It'll be okay, Maria," she signed, her voice filled with a conviction that belied her young age. "You're strong. You can do it."

Her words, so simple yet so powerful, brought a wave of unexpected comfort. In that moment, I realized that Jewel, despite her own struggles, was a source of strength, a beacon of hope in the darkness that threatened to consume me.

"Thank you, Bunny," I signed, my heart swelling with gratitude.

Jewel smiled, her face lighting up like the sun. "You're welcome, Maria," she signed, her fingers still a little clumsy but her enthusiasm shining through. "Now, tell me more about this surgery!"

And so, I did. I switched between signing and scribbling notes on my notepad, making sure she understood everything. I told her about Dr. Berke, about the revolutionary new procedure, about the hope and fear that battled within me. Jewel listened intently, her eyes wide with wonder, her hands occasionally interrupting to ask a question or offer a word of encouragement, sometimes in sign, sometimes with her voice.

• • •

It felt good to share this with her, to have someone to talk to, even if the conversation was a bit fragmented. Jewel, with her usual boundless energy, peppered me with questions.

"Will it hurt?" she signed, her brow furrowed with worry.

"Maybe a little," I wrote on the pad, "but they give you medicine, so you don't feel it."

"Will you sound like a robot?" she asked, her voice full of childish curiosity.

I chuckled and signed, "No, silly. I'll sound

like me."

"But... what if it doesn't work?" she signed
slowly, her expression turning serious.

I hesitated, unsure how to answer that
question. The fear of failure, of remaining trapped
in this silent world, was a constant shadow in my
mind.

"I don't know," I admitted, writing the words
slowly on the pad. "But I kind of want to try."

Jewel nodded; her expression resolute. "I
know you'll be okay, Maria," she signed
confidently. "You're the strongest person I know."

Her words, spoken with such unwavering faith, brought a lump to my throat. In that moment, I realized that Jewel, despite her young age, saw something in me that I didn't always see in myself – a strength, a resilience, a determination to overcome any obstacle.

And as I looked at her, her bright eyes shining with unwavering belief, I knew that I couldn't let her down. I had to fight for my voice, not just for myself, but for Jewel, for all the people who had been silenced by circumstance, by fear, by the cruelty of the world.

As we talked, I noticed a familiar figure

across the street. The mystery man. He was leaning against a lamppost, his gaze fixed on us, his expression unreadable.

Jewel followed my gaze and waved enthusiastically. "Hey, Ashwin!" she shouted, her voice carrying across the street.

The man, Ashwin, looked up, startled, then smiled and crossed the street towards us.

"Ashwin, this is my friend Maria," Jewel signed, her fingers moving with practiced ease. "She's the one I told you about, the one who's teaching me to sign."

Ashwin's eyes met mine, and a warmth spread through me, erasing the lingering chill of fear. His gaze was kind, understanding, and filled with a quiet strength that resonated deep within me.

"It's nice to meet you, Maria," he signed, his movements a bit hesitant, but his smile genuine.

"Nice to meet you too," I signed back, a shy smile curving my lips.

We sat there for a while, the three of us, bathed in the warm glow of the streetlights, our conversation a mix of signed and spoken words, a testament to the power of communication, of connection, of friendship.

• • •

As the night deepened, and Jewel's parents called her in, I felt a sense of peace settle over me. The fear was still there, lurking in the shadows, but it no longer held the same power. I had found strength in the most unexpected places – in the unwavering support of my father, in the innocent wisdom of a child, and in the quiet presence of a stranger who, in that moment, felt like a friend.

And as I watched Ashwin walk away, his silhouette disappearing into the night, I knew that I wasn't alone in this journey. I had people who cared, people who believed in me, people who would be there for me, no matter what the future held. And with that knowledge, a renewed sense of hope bloomed within me, a hope that whispered of a future where my silence could be broken, where my voice could finally be heard.

Chapter 6

The late summer breeze carried the scent of jasmine through El Centro de Oro as I embarked on my secret mission. A plan was brewing in my mind, a desperate attempt to counter the darkness that had fallen over Jewel's life. If she wasn't going to have a party, then I would give her one - a surprise so grand it would chase away the shadows, if only for a day.

The first step was the dress. I remembered Jewel's eyes shining as she described the ones she saw on TV, the ones worn by the girls who had parties and presents and happy families. I was determined to find her one even better, something that would make her feel like the princess she deserved to be.

With a mischievous grin, I pulled out the wad of bills Papi gave me every month. It was money to spend on whatever I wanted. I carefully counted the bills and tucked them away in a tin box under my bed. It wasn't much, but it was enough for a dress, a small detective cake with a bunny on it, and maybe even a few extra treats.

The next day, I ventured into the heart of El Centro de Oro, my senses alive with the vibrant energy of my neighborhood. The market was a kaleidoscope of colors, the stalls overflowing with fabrics of every texture and pattern imaginable.

I carefully made my way through the market stalls, my fingers trailing over fabrics - silks and cottons, sequins and lace. Each vendor greeted me with familiar warmth, some using the basic signs they'd learned over the years of my shopping there.

Finally, I found it. A dress of shimmering turquoise, adorned with delicate lace and tiny beads that sparkled like stars. It was perfect - not too formal but special enough to make Jewel feel like the princess she deserved to be.

As word of my plan spread through the neighborhood, more people stepped forward to help. The elderly couple who ran the flower shop offered to provide centerpieces. The local musician who played in the plaza volunteered to bring his guitar. Even the stern librarian who had often shushed Jewel's excited chatter softened, promising to contribute some books as presents.

Ashwin proved to be an invaluable ally. His quiet determination matched my own, and his strategic mind helped refine our plans. He suggested using his townhome as the staging area for decorations and presents, knowing Jewel would never suspect.

The night before the party, I lay awake in bed, my mind racing through every detail. The turquoise dress hung in my closet, wrapped in tissue paper. The cake was ordered, the decorations were hidden, and the guests were sworn to secrecy. Yet anxiety gnawed at my stomach. What if Ashley and Ted found out? What if they punished Jewel for having fun? What if this moment of joy only made her reality harder to bear?

Morning would come soon enough, bringing with it either triumph or disaster. But as I finally drifted toward sleep, I held onto one truth: Jewel deserved this celebration, this moment of normalcy and happiness. Whatever consequences came, we would face them together.

The party was more than just a celebration - it was a promise. A silent vow to protect Jewel, to show her that she was loved, that she deserved a

childhood filled with joy and laughter, not pain and

fear. As I finally drifted off to sleep, the turquoise

dress catching moonlight in my closet, I knew that

this party was just the beginning. Whatever it took,

I would find a way to be her voice, her protector,

her safe harbor in the storm that was her life. It was

a promise I intended to keep, no matter the cost.

Chapter 7

Time seemed to slow down, each passing day a heavy weight on my chest. Jewel's clothes became progressively more worn, the same outfits reappearing with alarming frequency. The knot in my stomach tightened with each observation, a silent alarm bell ringing in the quiet spaces of my world.

Should I say something? Should I reach out to Jewel? The questions echoed unanswered, bouncing off the walls of my uncertainty. I was, after all, just Maria, the silent girl, the one who observed but rarely interfered.

Yet, something about Jewel's fading smile,

the slump of her shoulders that she tried to hide, tugged at my heart. It was a subtle shift, a dimming of her usual vibrant energy, but it was enough to set off alarm bells in my head.

I remembered the day I first saw her, a whirlwind of pigtails and boundless energy, a stark contrast to the quiet solitude I'd become accustomed to. Her laughter had filled the spaces of my silent world, her presence a comforting rhythm in the otherwise predictable symphony of my days.

But now, that laughter seemed less frequent, replaced by a quietness that mirrored my own. The realization hit me like a wave, leaving me breathless in the sudden understanding of the situation. Jewel, my bright and bubbly Bunny, was not okay.

The thought sent a shiver down my spine, a cold wave washing over me despite the warmth of the summer day. I had to do something. I had to help her. But what could I do? I was just Maria, the silent girl, the one who observed but rarely interfered.

Yet, a voice within me, a voice I hadn't heard in a long time, whispered a message of defiance. I couldn't stand by and watch Jewel fade away. I had to find a way to help her, to be her voice in a world that seemed determined to silence her.

● ● ●

The decision settled in my heart, a quiet determination taking root. I would be Jewel's protector, her advocate, her friend. I would find a way to break through the silence and help her find her own voice.

And I had. The party, just a few days ago, had been a resounding success. Seeing Jewel's face light up as she walked into Ashwin's townhouse, transformed into a birthday wonderland, filled me with a joy I hadn't felt in years. The memory of her laughter, her excitement, her heartfelt "thank you" echoed in my mind, a reminder that even small acts of kindness could make a big difference.

But the party was just a temporary respite, a

fleeting moment of happiness in a life that was otherwise filled with darkness. I knew that the underlying issues, the neglect, the abuse, were still there, lurking in the shadows.

Maybe it was time to rethink the surgery. Dr. Berke's words echoed in my mind: risky, experimental, a small chance of... death. But what if it was the key? What if finding my voice was the only way to truly protect Jewel, to speak up for her, to be the advocate she so desperately needed?

The thought sent a shiver down my spine, not of fear this time, but of determination. Maybe the risk was worth it. Maybe finding my voice wasn't just about me anymore. Maybe it was about

Jewel, about giving her a voice too, about breaking the silence that had allowed the darkness to fester for far too long.

"Maria, earth to Maria!" Jewel's voice cut through my thoughts, and she waved a hand in front of my face. I looked up to see her, a shadow of her usual vibrant self, standing before me.

My lips curved into a gentle smile as I signed, "Good morning, Bunny."

She gave me a hug, but it lacked the usual enthusiasm, the carefree abandon that had always been her trademark. I hugged her back, my concern deepening as I noticed the same faded dress she had worn yesterday, the same unkempt hair, the same shadows under her eyes.

My fingers danced to form the words, "Bunny, when is your birthday again?" I asked, chickening out at the last minute. I didn't want to hurt her feelings by asking insensitive questions.

She giggled, but it was a hollow sound, devoid of genuine joy. "In 14 days. I will be turning 8 years old."

"So soon," I signed. "Why didn't you tell me?"

"Mama said I am not having a party this

year because I am a bad girl," she whispered, her voice barely audible.

My heart broke. Jewel, the sweetest and kindest child I had ever met, believed she was bad, that she didn't deserve to be celebrated.

"What do you want for your birthday?" I signed. "I will get you anything you want."

Her eyes widened, a spark of hope flickering in their depths. "Anything?" she asked, her voice barely a whisper.

I nodded, my smile widening. "Anything," I confirmed, my fingers signing the word with a flourish.

She bit her lip, her brow furrowed in thought. Finally, she looked up at me, her eyes shining with a mixture of excitement and uncertainty. "I want a new dress," she whispered, her voice barely audible. "A pretty one, like the ones the girls on TV wear."

My heart ached for her. It was such a simple wish, yet it spoke volumes about the neglect she was facing. I knelt down in front of her, meeting her gaze. "You deserve a new dress, Bunny," I signed. "And a party. You deserve a party with balloons and cake and presents."

She gasped, her eyes widening in surprise. "But Mama said..." she began, her voice trailing off.

"Don't listen to her," I signed, my fingers flying across my palms. "You're a good girl, Bunny. You are kind and smart and funny, and you deserve to be celebrated."

A tear escaped her eye, and she quickly wiped it away. "Really?" she asked, her voice small and hopeful.

"Really," I confirmed, my smile soft and reassuring. "I'll make sure you have a birthday you'll never forget."

She launched herself into my arms, her hug tight and fierce. "Thank you, Maria," she mumbled into my shoulder. "You're the best friend ever."

I held her close, my heart swelling with a mix of sadness and determination. I would make sure Jewel had a birthday she deserved, a day filled with joy and laughter and love. It was a promise I intended to keep, no matter the cost.

But this time, it wouldn't just be a party. I would find a way to protect her, to be her voice, to shield her from the darkness that threatened to consume her. This time, I wouldn't let her down. And maybe, just maybe, I would find my own voice in the process.

● ● ●

Chapter 8

The day of the party dawned bright and sunny, the sky a clear, vibrant blue that mirrored the excitement bubbling within me. I woke up with a jolt, my heart pounding with a mix of anticipation and nerves. Today was the day. Today, I would give Jewel the surprise of her life, a birthday party filled with joy, laughter, and love.

I glanced at the clock. 6:00 AM. Jewel wouldn't be coming over until after school, which gave me plenty of time to put the finishing touches on my secret plan. I crept out of bed, careful not to wake Papi, and tiptoed to the living room.

"And where do you think you're going?"

Rose's voice cut through the silence, startling me.

I turned to see her standing in the hallway, her arms crossed, her expression a mix of suspicion and disapproval.

I quickly signed. "I'm going to the library." Hoping she would buy it.

Rose eyed me skeptically. "The library? At this hour?"

I nodded, trying to maintain a neutral expression, "I need to return some books."

Rose waved a dismissive hand, her attention

• • •

already back on the television. "Whatever," she mumbled, her eyes glued to the screen. "Just try not to make a mess."

I nodded and quickly made my way out of the apartment, relieved to have avoided further questioning.

Instead of heading to the library, I hurried across the street to Ashwin's townhouse. He had graciously offered his home for the party, knowing it would be the perfect surprise for Jewel. I found him in the kitchen, brewing a pot of coffee, a rare smile gracing his lips.

"Good morning, Maria," he signed, his

movements fluid and confident. "Ready for the big day?"

I nodded eagerly, my heart pounding with excitement.

The townhouse was transformed. Streamers of every color imaginable crisscrossed the ceiling, balloons bobbed merrily in the corners, and a giant "Happy Birthday" banner hung proudly on the wall. The detective cake with a bunny on it sat in the center of the table, its chocolate frosting glistening under the soft glow of the fairy lights.

I smiled, my heart swelling with satisfaction. It was perfect. A magical haven for my precious

Bunny, a world away from the darkness that had shrouded her life.

As the morning wore on, the excitement grew. Neighbors popped in with gifts and well wishes, their faces beaming with anticipation. Mrs. Rodriguez arrived with the cake; her smile as sweet as the chocolatey aroma that filled the air. Mr. Garcia brought a piñata, its colorful molded shell promising a shower of treats and laughter.

Even the stern librarian, Mrs. Peterson, made an appearance, her arms laden with books and a rare smile gracing her lips. "I thought Jewel might enjoy these," she said.

I thanked her, my heart warmed by the unexpected kindness. It seemed that everyone in El Centro de Oro had come together to celebrate Jewel, to create a moment of joy in the midst of the darkness that had touched her life.

As the afternoon wore on, my anticipation grew. I paced the apartment, checking and rechecking every detail, my fingers nervously fidgeting. Where was Jewel? Why wasn't she here yet?

Finally, I heard a knock on the door. My heart leaped in my chest. This was it. The moment I had been waiting for.

I took a deep breath, plastered a smile on my face, and opened the door.

And there she was. My precious Bunny, her eyes wide with surprise, her mouth agape.

"Happy birthday, Jewel!" I signed, my fingers dancing with excitement.

Jewel stared at the decorations, the cake, the presents, her face a picture of disbelief. Then, a slow smile spread across her face, transforming her features into a radiant sunbeam.

"Is this... for me?" she signed, her voice barely a whisper.

• • •

I nodded, my smile widening, signing. "Of course, Bunny. It's your special day."

Jewel's eyes filled with tears, and she launched herself into my arms, her hug tight and fierce. "Thank you, Maria," she sobbed, her voice muffled against my shoulder. "This is the best birthday ever."

I held her close, my own tears threatening to spill over. In that moment, all the fear, the anxiety, the uncertainty melted away, replaced by a wave of pure joy. I had done it. I had given Jewel the happiness she deserved, the love she craved, the moment of magic that would forever shine in her memory.

The party was a whirlwind of laughter, games, and music. Jewel, dressed in her new turquoise dress, was the radiant center of attention, her smile infectious, her laughter a melody that filled the air.

We played games, ate cake, and danced until we were breathless. Jewel's face was alight with joy, her eyes sparkling with a happiness I had rarely seen.

As the party wound down, and the guests began to leave, Jewel turned to me, her expression filled with gratitude.

"Thank you, Maria," she said, her voice thick with emotion. "This was the best day of my life."

I smiled, my heart overflowing with love for this precious child who had touched my life in ways I never could have imagined.

"You're welcome, Bunny," I signed. "I'm just glad I could make you happy."

Jewel hugged me tightly, then skipped off to her apartment, her laughter echoing in the hallway, a sweet melody that chased away the lingering shadows.

As I cleaned up the remnants of the party with Ashwin, a comfortable silence settled between us. We worked side-by-side, our movements in sync, a silent understanding passing between us.

"Thank you," I signed, my gaze meeting his. "For everything."

He smiled, his eyes crinkling at the corners. "It was my pleasure, Maria. Seeing Jewel so happy... it was worth it."

I nodded, my heart filled with gratitude for this unexpected friend, this quiet ally who had helped me bring a moment of joy into Jewel's life.

• • •

The party was a testament to the power of love, of friendship, of community. It was a beacon of hope in the darkness, a reminder that even in the face of adversity, joy could be found, laughter could be shared, and love could conquer all.

Chapter 9

The late autumn breeze carried the scent of
jasmine through El Centro de Oro as I watched
Jewel skip across the cracked pavement. Her energy
was infectious, a stark contrast to my silent world.
She had become a regular fixture in my life, her
visits as predictable as the sun rising each morning.
But lately, something had changed in the way she
moved, in the light behind her eyes.

I tried telling Rose Anderson about my
concerns. My hands would fly through signs,
desperately trying to convey the urgency of the
situation, but she would just wave me off with that
dismissive look I'd grown to hate. "Maria, dear,
you're imagining things," she would say slowly, as

if I couldn't hear. "Children get bruises all the time. Stop being so dramatic." Her disbelief was like a physical barrier, another wall in my silent prison.

It started with small things that most people might overlook. The same faded yellow dress appearing day after day, its hem fraying more with each wear. Her once-bouncy curls hung limp and unwashed. The worn-out shoes with holes developing in the soles. I noticed because I had learned to read the stories that bodies tell when voices can't or won't speak.

From my perch on the fire escape, I would watch her approach our building, studying how her movements changed depending on the day.

Sometimes she bounded up the steps like the bunny I'd nicknamed her after. Other days, she moved with a careful slowness that made my heart ache.

The bruises appeared gradually, like shadows creeping across a sunny day. First, it was a small mark on her arm, barely noticeable against her light brown skin with a golden undertone. Then came the fingerprint-shaped bruises on her wrist, the suspicious dark patches that her too-big clothes couldn't quite hide.

"I fell on the playground," became her mantra, delivered with a smile that never quite reached her eyes. But playgrounds don't leave marks shaped like adult hands, and jungle gyms don't explain the way she flinched when someone moved too quickly near her.

I began watching Ashley McMillan more closely. She would stumble up the street some evenings, her movements erratic, her eyes glazed. Other times, she seemed almost normal, chatting with neighbors as if nothing was wrong. But there was always something off, a darkness that lurked beneath her carefully maintained facade.

Ted McMillan was worse. His presence in the neighborhood was like a storm cloud, dark and threatening. When he was around, Jewel seemed to shrink into herself, becoming smaller, quieter, less like the bright spirit I had come to love.

• • •

One particularly hot afternoon, Jewel appeared at my door, her face tear-stained and her cheek sporting a fresh bruise that no playground could have caused. The mark was clearly a handprint, adult-sized and angry against her small face.

My hands trembled as I signed, "What happened, Bunny?"

She stood there, scuffing her worn shoe against the floor, her usual chatter silenced by whatever horror had transpired in her home. When she finally spoke, her voice was barely a whisper. "Mama was mad. She said I was being bad."

The words hit me like physical blows. I knelt before her, gently tilting her face up to meet my eyes. My fingers moved slowly, deliberately, "You can tell me the truth, Bunny. Did someone hurt you?"

A single tear escaped, cutting a path through the dirt on her cheek. The sight broke something inside me. I pulled her close, wishing I could absorb her pain, take away the fear that had no place in a child's eyes.

The whispers started then. Neighbors gathered in small groups, their voices hushed but their gestures animated. Police cars became regular visitors to our street, their lights painting the buildings in alternating red and blue. The sound of arguments and breaking glass from the McMillan apartment became a terrible lullaby for our neighborhood.

From across the street, I noticed the Ashwin watching too. His dark eyes would follow Jewel's progress up and down the street, his expression troubled. Sometimes our eyes would meet, and I could see my own concern reflected in his gaze.

Each day brought new worries. Jewel's stories became more elaborate, her excuses more desperate. "I ran into a door," she'd say, or "I fell down the stairs." But stairs don't leave perfect

• • •

circular bruises, and doors don't create patterns that look like belt marks.

I started documenting everything in a small notebook - dates, injuries, explanations. My hands shook as I wrote each entry, knowing these notes might someday be important but praying they'd never need to be used.

The guilt began to eat at me. Each night, I lay awake, replaying every interaction, every sign I might have missed. My silence, once a simple fact of my existence, became a crushing weight. How could I protect her when I couldn't even call out for help?

I tried to create a safe haven for her in my apartment. We would spend hours drawing, her chatter filling my silent world with color and life. I taught her sign language, and she soaked it up like a sponge, her small hands forming words with growing confidence.

Despite everything, Jewel's spirit remained remarkably unbroken. She still found joy in small things - a butterfly landing on the windowsill, a particularly pretty cloud, the way the setting sun turned the buildings golden. Her laughter, when it came, was still genuine, still pure.

But there were moments when the mask slipped, when the weight of her home life became too heavy for her small shoulders to bear. In those moments, she would curl up beside me on the fire escape, her head resting against my shoulder, and we would sit in shared silence, watching the world go by below.

As summer faded into autumn, the situation grew worse. The arguments from the McMillan apartment became more frequent, more violent. Jewel spent more time at my place, sometimes falling asleep on my couch, exhausted from carrying burdens no child should have to bear.

I tried to report what I was seeing. My hands flew through signs as I explained my concerns to anyone who would listen - teachers, neighbors, even the police when they responded to yet another disturbance call. But without a voice, without the ability to speak the words aloud, my warnings seemed to carry less weight.

I noticed Ashwin making his own calls, presumably to report what he was witnessing. But like my silent protests, his concerns seemed to disappear into the bureaucratic void.

One evening, as Jewel prepared to return home, she turned to me with eyes too old for her young face. "Maria," she said, her voice steady despite the tremor in her hands, "you're my best friend. You know that, right?"

I nodded, my heart breaking at the adult solemnity in her expression.

"Promise you'll always be my friend?" she asked, her small fingers forming the signs we'd practiced together.

"Always, Bunny," I signed back, pulling her into a tight hug. "Always."

I couldn't know then that this promise would haunt me, that it would become both a blessing and a curse. I couldn't know that my silence, my inability to speak up more forcefully, would become my greatest regret.

As I watched her walk away that evening, her small figure growing smaller against the setting sun, I felt a deep sense of foreboding. The shadows were growing longer, darker, and my precious Bunny was walking right into them.

The guilt of those moments, of every time I watched her return to that house of horrors, would stay with me forever. It would become the force that drove me to seek my voice, to fight against the silence that had allowed such darkness to flourish.

But for now, all I could do was watch, document, and pray that someone, somewhere, would hear the screams that my silence couldn't voice.

Chapter 10

Locked in my room, the muffled sounds of the outside world barely reached me. The walls seemed to close in around me, their faded paint and cracks a reflection of the isolation I felt. Papi had left for his shift at the hospital, and Rose Anderson, the nanny, had decided the best way to deal with a mute teenager was to simply lock her away. The air in the room was stale, heavy with the scent of old books and the faint trace of lavender from a forgotten sachet in the corner.

I lay in bed, staring at the ceiling, tracing the faint water stains that formed abstract shapes. My mind wandered, trying to escape the suffocating silence. I thought of the world outside, the laughter of children, the hum of life that I could no longer fully participate in. My hands itched to sign, to express the words trapped inside me, but there was no one to see, no one to understand.

A sudden thump jolted me from my thoughts. My heart raced as I sat up, straining to hear more. Then another thump, followed by screams that sent chills down my spine. Ashley, Jewel's mother voice, I realized with growing horror. My face was wet with tears before I even realized I was crying.

As I clutched my phone, my mind drifted to the first time I met Jewel. It was a sunny afternoon, and she had wandered into the small park where I often sought refuge. Her laughter had been infectious, a bright melody that seemed to cut through the noise of the world. She had approached me without hesitation, her wide, curious eyes taking in my silence with a kind of wonder.

"Why don't you talk?" she had asked, her voice filled with innocent curiosity. I smiled, pulling out my small notepad and pen to write my response. "I can't," I had written, showing her the words.

She frowned for a moment, then brightened. "That's okay. I can talk enough for both of us!" she had declared, plopping down beside me on the bench. From that day on, she had become a constant presence in my life, her boundless energy and

chatter filling the spaces where my voice could not.

With trembling fingers, I dialed 911. The

voice that answered was calm, professional, but it

felt distant, like a lifeline just out of reach.

"911 operator speaking." I began frantically

pressing the number keys, each press felt like a

scream in the void, a desperate attempt to bridge the

gap between my silence and her understanding.

"911 operator speaking, is someone there?"

The voice came again, this time with a hint of

urgency. I pressed harder, hoping she could

understand what I was trying to do.

"Can you not talk?" I pressed the key once more time. "Does that mean yes?" I pressed the key again, my heart pounding in my chest.

"Ok. I understand. Do you need help? Press once for yes and twice for no." I pressed once, the motion sharp and deliberate.

"Great. Are you hurt?" Her question hung in the air, and I hesitated. How could I explain that it wasn't me who was hurt? I pressed three times, hoping she would understand my confusion.

"I am not sure what that means. Is someone hurt?" I nodded instinctively, even though she couldn't see me, and pressed the key once.

"Okay. Is the person with you? Press 1 for yes, 2 for no." My hand hovered over the keypad. Jewel wasn't with me, but in a way, she was. I pressed 1, feeling a pang of guilt for the half-truth.

I thought of the times we had spent together, her small hand slipping into mine as we walked through the neighborhood, her laughter ringing out as she told me stories about her day. She had a way of making me feel seen, of reminding me that silence didn't have to mean invisibility.

"Can you tell me your address?" My stomach clenched. How could I? I couldn't speak.

Panic bubbled up, threatening to overwhelm me. I frantically pressed buttons, hoping to somehow convey my desperation.

"If you can't speak, try tapping on the phone. Do you know your address?" I tapped once, hard, the sound echoing in the silence of my room.

"Good. Can you tap out the numbers of your address slowly? Tap for each street address number?" she asked, her voice steady and reassuring. I took a deep breath, trying to calm myself. Focusing all my energy, I tapped the numbers of our apartment building, then the street number. Each tap felt like an eternity, the seconds stretching into hours.

The thought of Jewel, trapped in that house with Ashley and Ted, filled me with a sense of helplessness. I had to do something. I couldn't let her light be extinguished by the darkness that surrounded her.

"Stay on the line with me. Help is on its way," she said, her voice a lifeline in the chaos. But my heart continued to hammer against my ribs. Ashley's screams pierced the air again, raw and guttural, sending chills down my spine.

Then, another thump. Harder this time. A sob escaped my lips, and I clutched the phone tighter, as if it were the only thing tethering me to reality. I pressed my ear against the wall, desperate to hear something, anything, from Jewel. But there was only silence. A terrifying, suffocating silence that seemed to mock my helplessness.

The minutes stretched like hours as I waited, each second marked by the frantic beating of my heart. The operator's voice continued to reassure me, but her words seemed to come from far away, drowned out by the sound of blood rushing in my ears and the echo of those terrible screams.

Chapter 11

The pounding on my apartment door jolted me from my desperate vigil by the phone. Voices - authoritative, urgent - filtered through the walls. Police. They were here. My heart leaped as I heard Rose Anderson's measured tones responding to them.

"Yes, officers? How can I help you?"

I launched myself at my bedroom door, my fists hammering against the wood. The impact sent shockwaves of pain through my hands, but I didn't care. I had to make them hear me. Had to make them understand.

• • •

"There's someone in there?" A male voice asked sharply.

"Oh, that's just Maria, the doctor's daughter. She's... difficult to manage sometimes."

My blood boiled at her casual dismissal. I slammed harder against the door, my movements becoming frantic.

Suddenly, the voice was closer. "Miss? Stand back from the door."

I stumbled backward just as the door burst open. Two officers stood there, their expressions shifting from concern to confusion to understanding as they took in my locked bedroom and tear-stained face.

"She's deaf," Rose offered from behind them, as if that explained everything.

I signed, furiously, "I'm mute, stupid."

The female officer's face hardened as she turned to Rose. "You locked her in?"

While they dealt with Rose, the male officer gestured for me to follow him outside. I could barely breathe as we descended the stairs, my legs trembling beneath me. A female officer met us at the bottom, her kind eyes full of sympathy as she guided me to sit on the steps, away from the growing crowd.

"Stay here," she signed haltingly, surprising me. I nodded, wrapping my arms around myself as I watched the scene unfold across the street.

More emergency vehicles arrived, their lights painting the neighborhood alternating red and blue. A crowd had gathered, their faces grave. I spotted him then - Ashwin, his dark eyes fixed on the McMillan's door with an expression of dawning horror.

And then I understood.

The stretcher emerged first; its small burden covered by a white sheet. Too small. Too still. My heart refused to accept what my eyes were telling me, even as my body moved of its own accord. I was running before I realized it, a silent scream building in my chest, a scream that would never find its voice.

Behind the stretcher came Ashley and Ted McMillan, their faces a study in contrasts - her tear-streaked, his coldly defiant, both with hands cuffed behind their backs. The sight of them - these people who had been trusted to protect and love their child - ignited something primal within me. My vision blurred with rage at seeing Ashley's theatrical tears and Ted's calculating stare, knowing how they had betrayed that sacred trust.

A silent guttural scream tore through my
body as I watched them wheel out Bunny's broken
form. My precious Jewel, the little girl who had
brought such light into my silent world, lay
motionless beneath stark white sheets. My legs
carried me forward even as my mind begged to run
away, to wake up from this nightmare. My
trembling hand reached out; my honey-gold eyes
wide with desperate denial. This couldn't be real.
Any moment now, Bunny would bounce up with
that radiant smile that had earned her nickname, her
energy infectious as always.

With shaking fingers, I pulled back the

covers, and my world shattered completely. Those sparkling green eyes, which had always danced with mischief, were now closed forever. The golden curls, usually bouncing with every movement, lay still and lifeless against the stark white sheet. That beautiful face that had beamed at me just yesterday was now marred by blood and bruises, telling the horrific story of her final moments. My Bunny lay silent and still, her boundless energy forever extinguished. Gone was the child who had accepted my silence without question, who had filled our shared moments with enough chatter and laughter for us both. In her place lay this broken shell, this cruel reminder of how merciless the world could be to its most innocent souls.

Around me, people turned away, unable to bear witness to my anguish. The scream building in my chest had nowhere to go, trapped like everything else in my silent world.

I lunged for Ashley, my hands reaching for her throat, but strong arms caught me from behind. I struggled against the grip, my body convulsing with rage and grief. It was him – Ashwin - holding me back, his embrace both restraining and comforting as I collapsed against him.

"This won't bring her back," Ashwin whispered, his voice a low rumble against my back. Though the words were lost to me, I felt the vibration of his voice, the compassion in his grip.

My legs gave out, and we sank to the ground together. He didn't let go, and I was grateful. Without his support, I might have shattered completely.

The female officer who had signed to me earlier approached, her face gentle. She knelt beside us and waited until I could focus on her hands.

"Do you want to see her? To say goodbye?" she signed.

I nodded, though every fiber of my being screamed in protest. Ashwin - my silent guardian - helped me to my feet, but stepped back as the officer led me to the stretcher.

A sob tore through me, silent but powerful enough to shake my entire body. My fingers traced the air above her face, signing the words I had never said enough: "I love you, Bunny."

Around me, people turned away, unable to bear witness to my anguish. The scream building in my chest had nowhere to go, trapped like everything else in my silent world. My hands, which had so often signed stories and love for my precious Bunny, hung uselessly at my sides. The crowd watched in respectful silence as I said my goodbye. Some were crying openly, while others turned away, unable to bear witness to such raw grief. Ashwin stood nearby, his presence a steady anchor in a world that had suddenly lost all meaning. There would be no more conversations between us, no more shared secrets, no more gentle hugs. No more anything.

As they prepared to take her away, I felt a gentle touch on my shoulder. The female officer again, her signs careful and clear.

"We need to ask you some questions. About Jewel. About what you heard."

I nodded, though the thought of reliving those moments made me physically ill. But I would do it. For Jewel. I would find a way to tell them everything - every scream, every thump, every moment I had spent trapped behind that locked door while she needed me.

Ashwin stepped forward then, his movements hesitant. He pulled out his phone, typed something quickly, and showed it to me:

"I'm here if you need someone to stay with you."

I stared at him through tears, this stranger who had become an unexpected source of comfort in my darkest moment. Slowly, I nodded, confusion battling with gratitude. Why hadn't he just spoken? Was he shy? Or was there something more to his silence?

As they wheeled Jewel's body away, I felt something inside me break and reform. The silence that had once been my prison now felt like a sanctuary, holding within it every laugh, every story, every precious moment I had shared with my Bunny. In this silence, she would live forever, dancing through my memories with the boundless energy that had made her so special.

The world continued to move around us - police documenting the scene, neighbors whispering among themselves, Ashley being placed in a patrol car - but I remained still, supported by this quiet stranger, my hands forming one last message to the

● ● ●

sky:

"Goodbye, my sweet Bunny. I'm sorry I couldn't save you."

And beneath that apology, another layer of guilt and grief settled in my heart. It was time. Time to face the surgery I had been putting off for far too long. The surgery that could restore my voice or steal my life.

Maybe, just maybe, if I had found my voice sooner, I could have been louder, clearer. Maybe I could have reached Jewel, could have given her the words she needed to hear, the words that might have saved her.

● ● ●

But those were maybes, whispers of a could-have-been world that haunted the silence of my reality. Now, all that remained was the decision, the surgery, the chance to break free from the chains of my past or be forever bound to them in the silence of death."

Chapter 12

The police station was a cold, sterile place, the walls painted a depressing shade of beige that seemed to absorb all the light and joy from the world. The air was thick with the scent of stale coffee and disinfectant, a pungent combination that made my stomach churn.

I sat in a small, windowless room, the only furniture a metal table and two uncomfortable chairs. Across from me sat the female officer who had signed to me earlier, her name tag reading "Officer Davis." Her kind eyes held a professional distance, but there was a flicker of understanding in their depths that gave me a sliver of comfort.

The officer's hands moved with a practiced grace in ASL as she began, "Hello, I'm Officer Davis. Can you tell me your name?"

I smiled slightly, signing back, "You don't need to sign, Officer. I can hear. I just can't talk."

Her eyebrows rose in surprise, but she quickly recovered. "Of course. My apologies," she said, her voice taking on a gentler tone. "Can you tell me your full name, please?"

I signed my name, "Maria Carmichael".

"Understood, Maria," she replied, her gaze steady and kind. "I know this is difficult, but we need to ask you some questions about Jewel."

I nodded, steeling myself for the ordeal.

"Can you tell me about the sounds you heard coming from the McMillans' apartment?" she asked, her voice gentle but firm.

My hands flew across the space between us, describing the muffled screams, the thumps and crashes that had punctuated the silence of my world. I recounted the fear I had felt, the helplessness of being trapped in my room, unable to help my little friend.

Officer Davis's brow furrowed as she

absorbed my words. "Can you be more specific about the timing of these sounds? Were they regular occurrences?"

Each question forced me to relive the trauma, to sift through the fragments of memory and piece together a timeline of horror. I remembered the nights punctuated by Jewel's muffled cries, the mornings when she'd arrive with fresh bruises, her smile strained.

"There was a pattern," I signed, my fingers trembling. "Especially when..." I hesitated, the memory of Jewel confiding in me about her mother's "bad days" flashing through my mind. The days when Ashley would disappear into her room, the bottle her only companion, leaving Jewel to fend for herself.

Officer Davis's eyes sharpened. "Especially when what, Maria?"

I took a deep breath, the guilt washing over me. "When her mother drank," I signed, shame burning in my throat.

The officer's expression hardened. "Did you ever see any signs of physical abuse?"

I closed my eyes, the image of Jewel's small, bruised arm flashing before me. The time she had fallen on the playground, she'd said. But the shape of the bruise, the way she flinched when I touched it... it hadn't looked like a playground injury.

"Yes," I signed, my fingers heavy with the weight of my confession. "But she always had an excuse."

The interrogation stretched on, each question a fresh stab of guilt, each detail a reminder of my own helplessness. Why hadn't I seen the signs sooner? Why hadn't I done more?

The door opened, and my father rushed in, his face etched with worry. He knelt beside me, his arms enveloping me in a tight embrace.

• • •

"Maria, mi amor," he whispered, his voice thick with emotion. "Are you alright?"

I clung to him, my body shaking with sobs. In that moment, I needed his comfort, his strength, his love.

When I finally calmed down, I looked up at him, my eyes filled with a newfound determination.

"Papi," I signed, my face showing determination, "it's time. I want the surgery."

My father's eyes widened in surprise. "Maria, are you sure?" he asked, his voice laced with concern. "It's a risky procedure. There's no guarantee..."

I cut him off, my hands signing with a firmness I had never displayed before. "I know, Papi. But I can't live like this anymore. I need my voice. I need to speak. Maybe then I could have saved her."

My father looked at me, his eyes searching mine, his heart heavy with the weight of his own fears and anxieties. But he also saw the determination in my eyes, the strength that had been forged in the fires of loss and silence.

He nodded slowly, his voice a whisper of acceptance. "Okay, mi amor. We'll do it. We'll get your voice back."

I smiled, a glimmer of hope shining through the tears. It was time. Time to face the unknown, to embrace the risk, to fight for the voice that had been stolen from me. It was time to break the silence, to reclaim my life, to honor the memory of my sweet Bunny, who had taught me the power of words, the beauty of connection, the strength of love.

As we left the interrogation room, I saw Ashwin again. He stood by the waiting area, his expression a mix of concern and something else I couldn't quite decipher. He caught my eye and offered a small, hesitant smile. In that moment, amidst the sterile coldness of the police station and the crushing weight of grief, his presence was a small beacon of warmth, a reminder that I wasn't alone.

The investigation continued, each new piece of evidence a hammer blow to my already fragile heart. The police uncovered a history of abuse, of neglect, of missed opportunities to save Jewel. The neighborhood, once a place of comfort and familiarity, now felt tainted, the whispers and sideways glances a constant reminder of the tragedy that had unfolded.

But through it all, there was Ashwin. The young man who watched from across the street, whose name I had learned but had never spoken. He listened without judgment, and in his own quiet way, was helping me find my voice again.

Chapter 13

The Los Angeles skyline blurred through the airplane window, a tapestry of steel and glass against a hazy sunset. Beside me, Papi sat rigid, his jaw clenched, his gaze fixed on the passing clouds. The silence between us was thick with unspoken anxieties, a stark contrast to the bustling city below. His surgeon's hands, usually so steady in the operating room, fidgeted with his seat belt, betraying his inner turmoil.

We were returning to UCLA Medical Center, this time not for a consultation, but for the surgery that could change my life forever. Dr. Berke's revolutionary procedure loomed ahead - a complex combination of stem cell therapy and

• • •

microsurgical reconstruction that could either restore my voice or... I pushed the darker thoughts away.

The pre-surgery consultations were a blur of medical terminology and sterile procedures. Dr. Berke's voice remained calm and reassuring as he walked us through each step: the harvesting of stem cells, the careful removal of scarred tissue, the delicate implantation of lab-grown vocal cords. Each explanation was accompanied by detailed diagrams that made my throat ache in anticipation.

"A very small chance of... death."

The words echoed in my mind, a chilling

reminder of the fragility of life. I touched my throat, feeling the scar tissue that had silenced me since the accident that took Mama. Would this surgery reunite me with her voice, or with her spirit?

But then, another image surfaced, pushing back the darkness. Jewel's smiling face, her bright eyes shining with mischief, her laughter echoing through the corridors of my memory. "You're the strongest person I know," she had signed, her small fingers moving with such conviction. Her faith in me had been absolute, unwavering - even in the face of her own struggles.

The night before the surgery, I found myself drawn to the hospital's garden, a poor substitute for my fire escape sanctuary. The city lights twinkled below, a symphony of urban life that I could only observe from the sidelines. My phone buzzed again. Another message from Ashwin: "Can't sleep?"

I smiled faintly, typing back: "Too many thoughts."

"Want to talk about it?"

My fingers hovered over the keyboard. Even in text, words sometimes felt inadequate. "I'm scared," I finally admitted. "Not just of the surgery. Of what comes after."

"What do you mean?"

"If I get my voice back... what if I don't know how to use it? What if I'm not the person everyone expects me to be?"

There was a long pause before his response appeared: "You'll be exactly who you are, Maria. Your voice doesn't define you - it's just another way to share who you've always been."

I blinked back tears, his words touching something deep within me. "I wish Jewel could see me after. She always wanted to hear my voice."

"She knew your voice already," he replied. "She heard it in your kindness, your strength, your love for her. The surgery won't give you a voice -

it'll just let others hear what she already knew was

there."

His words wrapped around me like a warm

blanket, offering comfort in the cold hospital

garden. "Thank you, Ashwin. For everything."

"Get some rest, Maria. Tomorrow is just the

beginning."

I clutched the phone to my chest, drawing

strength from his quiet confidence, before heading

back to my room to face whatever tomorrow would

bring.

The morning of the surgery arrived with the harsh fluorescent glare of hospital lights. As the anesthesiologist prepared the IV, I caught Papi's eye. His face was pale but resolute as he held my hand. "Te amo, mi amor," he whispered, it was something mama always said. Since her death papi has taken over speaking Spanish to me. His voice is thick with emotion. "Fight for your voice."

As consciousness began to fade, I thought of Jewel - her infectious laugh, her resilient spirit, her tragic end. Finding my voice wasn't just about me anymore. It was about speaking for those who couldn't, about breaking the silence that had allowed tragedy to flourish.

The last thing I saw before darkness claimed me was Jewel's face, her smile a beacon guiding me toward whatever lay ahead. For her, for myself, for all the words left unspoken - I would face this challenge. It was time to break free from the prison of silence.

Chapter 14

The sterile scent of the recovery room was the first thing that pierced through the haze of anesthesia. My eyes fluttered open, confusion clouding my vision. A white ceiling, the blurred outline of a figure leaning over me, and a dull ache throbbing in my throat.

"Maria, mi amor, you're awake," Papi's voice, thick with emotion, broke through the fog. His face, etched with worry lines that seemed to have deepened in the past few hours, swam into focus. His eyes, red-rimmed and filled with tears of relief, met mine.

I tried to speak, to reassure him, but only a

croak escaped my lips. The surgery had been a success, but my voice was still a fragile instrument, a newborn bird struggling to find its song.

The following days were a blur of pain, discomfort, and the constant struggle to swallow, to speak, to reclaim the voice that had been stolen from me. The physical challenges of recovery were immense, but they paled in comparison to the emotional turmoil that raged within me.

I spent hours in voice therapy, my tongue stumbling over unfamiliar sounds, my throat aching with the effort. The frustration was immense, the desire to speak warring with the limitations of my healing body.

But through it all, there was Ashwin. He had flown over as soon as the surgery ended, his presence a calming force in the sterile environment of the hospital. He listened patiently as I struggled to form words, his smile encouraging, his eyes filled with unwavering belief.

And there were the memories of Jewel, her laughter echoing in my mind, her words a constant source of inspiration.

"You're the strongest person I know," she had signed, her small fingers firm and resolute.

Her belief in me fueled my determination. I

wouldn't let her down. I wouldn't let the pain, the frustration, the fear, defeat me. I would find my voice, for her, for myself, for all those who had been silenced.

One afternoon, as I sat in my hospital bed, staring out the window at the bustling city below, a wave of grief washed over me. The realization that my newfound voice couldn't bring Jewel back, that it couldn't erase the pain she had endured, hit me with the force of a physical blow.

Tears streamed down my face, my silent sobs echoing in the quiet room. Ashwin, sensing my distress, rushed to my side, his hand gently resting on my shoulder.

"It's okay, Maria," he said, his voice soft and reassuring. "You're doing great. Just take it one day at a time."

I looked at him, my heart filled with gratitude for his unwavering support. He understood, without needing an explanation, the complicated emotions that swirled within me - the hope, the grief, the guilt, the determination.

And as I looked at him, I realized that my voice wasn't just for Jewel, it was for me too. It was for the chance to connect with others, to express my thoughts and feelings, to reclaim my place in the world.

• • •

It was then, in the quiet solitude of my hospital room, that I made a promise to myself, a vow to honor Jewel's memory. I would use my voice to speak for those who couldn't, to be an advocate for the voiceless, to fight for justice and protection for all children.

I would become the voice of the forgotten, the silenced, the abused. I would be their champion, their protector, their hope.

That night, I picked up my pen and notebook, the words flowing effortlessly onto the page. It was a song for Jewel, a tribute to her innocence, her resilience, her unwavering spirit.

(Verse 1)

She walks to school with her head held
down

She hides the bruises with her long brown
hair

She prays that this day will be better than
the last

But her mama's passed out and her daddy's
gone

(Chorus)

A concrete angel, with wings of dust

Slips through the cracks, unnoticed and
unloved

Her cries for help, unheard and unseen

A silent tragedy, a life that could have been

The song poured out of me, a melody of grief and hope, of loss and love. It was a tribute to Jewel, a promise to keep her memory alive, a vow to fight for a world where no child would suffer in silence.

The next day, during my voice therapy session, a breakthrough came. As I struggled to pronounce a particularly difficult word, a sound emerged, clear and strong. It was my voice, my own voice, speaking after years of silence.

Tears welled up in my eyes, not tears of sadness this time, but tears of joy, of triumph, of hope. I had done it. I had found my voice.

The journey ahead was still long, the road to full recovery paved with challenges and setbacks. But in that moment, as my voice echoed in the small therapy room, I knew that I had taken the first step, a step towards healing, towards self-discovery, towards a future where my voice could finally be heard.

And as I sang Jewel's song, my voice filled with emotion, I knew that she was listening, her spirit soaring on the wings of my newfound voice, her memory forever etched in my heart.

Chapter 15

The warm Philadelphia sun streamed

through the windows of my childhood bedroom in El Centro de Oro, casting a golden glow on the faded posters and dusty shelves. It had been six months since the surgery, six months of intense therapy and grueling practice. Six months of rediscovering my voice, of learning to shape sounds into words, words into sentences, sentences into songs.

I stood before the mirror, studying my reflection. The scar on my throat had faded to a thin white line, barely visible unless you knew where to look. But the changes went far deeper than skin. My eyes, once shadowed with fear and uncertainty, now held a quiet determination. I was no longer the silent observer, trapped in a world without sound. I was Maria Carmichael, and I had a voice.

With trembling fingers, I reached for the small box on my dresser. Inside lay a delicate silver necklace, a tiny bunny charm dangling from its chain. I had bought it for Jewel, its delicate turquoise jewel eyes sparkling in the light. It was meant to be her favorite, a gift to make her feel special and loved. Now, it served as a bittersweet reminder of the little girl who had brought so much light into my silent world.

As I fastened the necklace around my throat, I thought of Jewel. Her laughter, her boundless energy, her unwavering faith in me. "You're the strongest person I know," she had signed. Those words had become my mantra, pushing me through

the darkest days of recovery.

A soft knock at the door pulled me from my

reverie. "Maria?" Papi's voice, warm and hesitant.

"Are you ready?"

I took a deep breath, my hand instinctively

reaching for the bunny charm. "Yes," I said, my

voice still slightly raspy but growing stronger every

day. "I'm ready."

Papi's eyes widened slightly at the sound of

my voice, a mix of pride and lingering disbelief

crossing his face. Even after all these months,

hearing me speak was still a novelty, a miracle he

couldn't quite believe.

We drove in silence, the familiar streets of El Centro de Oro passing by in a blur. So much had changed, yet so much remained the same. The bodega where Jewel and I used to buy candy still stood on the corner, its faded awning fluttering in the breeze. Children played on the sidewalks, their laughter a bittersweet reminder of what we had lost.

As we approached the community center, I saw a crowd gathering. Familiar faces from the neighborhood, police officers, social workers, and... Ashwin. He stood apart from the others, his dark eyes finding mine as we pulled up. A small smile played on his lips, encouraging and warm.

I stepped out of the car, my knees weak but my resolve strong. This was it. The moment I had been preparing for. The reason I had fought so hard to reclaim my voice.

The room fell silent as I approached the podium, all eyes on me. I cleared my throat, my fingers brushing against the delicate silver necklace with the tiny bunny charm dangling from its chain. Its turquoise jewel eyes sparkled, giving me courage.

"My name is Maria Carmichael," I began, my voice clear and steady. "And I'm here to speak for those who can't speak for themselves."

• • •

As I shared Jewel's story, our story, I saw tears in the eyes of the audience. I spoke of the signs we had missed, the cries for help that went unheard, the system that had failed to protect an innocent child. My voice wavered at times, thick with emotion, but I pushed on, drawing strength from the memory of Jewel's unwavering belief in me.

"But this isn't just about Jewel," I continued, my voice growing stronger with each word. "It's about all the children living in silence, trapped in homes where love has been replaced by fear. It's about breaking that silence, about giving them a voice."

I outlined my proposal for a new community watch program, one that would train neighbors, teachers, and community members to recognize the signs of abuse. One that would provide a safe haven for children in need, a place where they could find help and hope. And most importantly, we will listen. We will hear the silent cries for help, and we will act."

As I spoke, I noticed a small butterfly landing on the window sill behind the audience. Its delicate wings were a brilliant turquoise, reminiscent of Jewel's eyes. For a moment, I faltered, overcome by the symbolism. But then I remembered Jewel's words: "You're the strongest person I know." I took a deep breath and continued, my voice steady and resolute.

As I finished speaking, the room erupted in applause. People stood, their faces a mix of determination and hope. I had done it. I had used my voice to make a difference.

Ashwin was the first to reach me as I stepped down from the podium. Without a word, he pulled me into a tight embrace. "I'm so proud of you," he whispered, his voice thick with emotion. "There's something I need to show you."

As we pulled apart, I saw Papi approaching, tears streaming down his face. "Mi amor," he said, enveloping me in his arms. "Your mama would be so proud."

I closed my eyes, letting the love and support wash over me. In that moment, I felt Jewel's presence, her spirit dancing around us, her laughter echoing in my heart.

Ashwin gently took my hand, leading me to a corner of the community center I hadn't noticed before. There, on the wall, was a beautifully crafted plaque. "Silent Symphony Foundation," it read, "In memory of Jewel McMillan."

My breath caught in my throat as Ashwin explained, "I wanted to do something to honor

Jewel's memory. This foundation will provide resources and support for children who are victims of abuse. It's a way to ensure that her story continues to be heard."

Tears welled up in my eyes as I traced the letters of Jewel's name on the plaque. "Ashwin," I whispered, my voice trembling with emotion, "this is beautiful. Thank you."

Ashwin's eyes met mine, a mix of nervousness and determination in his gaze. "Maria, there's something else I need to tell you," he said, his voice soft but steady. "I know this might not be the best time, but life is too short to leave things unsaid. I've always been interested in you, ever since I first saw you writing on that fire escape. Jewel used to tell me stories about you, and I fell for the woman in those stories long before I even spoke to you."

I stood there, stunned by his confession, my heart racing. Ashwin continued, "I understand if now isn't the right time for you, but I wanted you to know. No matter what you decide, I'll be here, supporting you every step of the way."

The road ahead would be long and challenging. There would be setbacks, obstacles, and moments of doubt. But I was ready. I had found my voice, and with the Silent Symphony Foundation and Ashwin by my side, we would

• • •

ensure that no child's cry for help would go unheard again.

As we left the community center, hand in hand with Ashwin and Papi, I looked up at the clear blue sky. "This is for you, Bunny," I whispered, my voice carried away by the gentle breeze. "I promise, your story will be heard."

And with that promise, I stepped forward into a future full of hope, determination, and the power of a voice reclaimed. As we left the community center, hand in hand with Ashwin and Papi, a comfortable silence settled over us. It was a silence filled with understanding, with shared grief, and with the quiet determination to honor Jewel's memory.

A few weeks later, as the autumn wind whispered through the trees, scattering golden leaves across the freshly turned earth of Jewel's grave, I stood there alone, my newly recovered voice still raw with emotion. I clutched a small bouquet of wildflowers, the same kind Jewel used to pick on our walks through the neighborhood.

Taking a deep breath, Maria began to sing. Her voice, though still hesitant, carried a haunting beauty as it floated through the quiet cemetery. The melody spoke of a young girl's struggles, of bruises hidden and prayers unanswered. It painted a picture of a vibrant spirit dimmed too soon, a precious jewel lost in the gloom of neglect and abuse.

(Verse 1)

She walks to school with her head held
down

She hides the bruises with her long brown
hair

She prays that this day will be better than
the last

But her mama's passed out and her daddy
don't care

(Chorus)

A vibrant spirit, dimmed too soon

A jewel so bright, lost in the gloom

Her cries for help, unheard and unseen

A silent tragedy, a life that could have been

As Maria sang, tears streamed down her face. Her voice grew stronger with each verse, infused with the pain of loss and the fierce love she felt for her young friend. The chorus, repeated with growing intensity, lamented the tragedy of Jewel's unheard cries for help and the life that could have been.

(Verse 2)

She sits in class, her mind a million miles away

The teacher's words, a distant, muffled drone

She dreams of a world where she's safe and free

But the bell rings, and it's back to reality

(Chorus)

A vibrant spirit, dimmed too soon

A jewel so bright, lost in the gloom

Her cries for help, unheard and unseen

A silent tragedy, a life that could have been

The song touched on the failures of those

who should have protected Jewel - the system that

let her slip through the cracks, the adults who turned

a blind eye. Maria's voice cracked as she sang of a

child's innocence lost, of silent screams and

desperate pleas that went unnoticed.

As she reached the final verses, Maria's

voice soared. She sang of freedom and release, imagining Jewel's spirit soaring beyond the reach of harm. The song concluded with a bittersweet tribute to the vibrant spirit that would forever remain a jewel in the hearts of those who loved her.

(Bridge)

The system fails, the cracks widen

A child's innocence, lost and broken

A silent scream, a desperate plea

But no one hears, no one sees

(Chorus)

A vibrant spirit, dimmed too soon

A jewel so bright, lost in the gloom

Her cries for help, unheard and unseen

A silent tragedy, a life that could have been

(Outro)

Fly away, little angel, fly away

Your pain is gone, your spirit free

Soar above the clouds, beyond the reach of

harm

A vibrant spirit, a jewel in our hearts

The last note faded into the autumn air, leaving behind a profound silence. Maria knelt and placed the wildflowers on Jewel's grave. "Goodbye, my sweet Bunny," she whispered, her voice hoarse from singing and emotion. "I promise, your story will be heard. Your life mattered, and I'll make sure the world knows it."

Rising slowly, Maria turned to leave the cemetery. She found Ashwin waiting at a respectful distance, his eyes filled with compassion. As they walked away together, Maria felt a mix of grief and determination. Her journey to reclaim her voice had been about more than just herself - it was about becoming a voice for the voiceless, a champion for children like Jewel.

With each step, Maria's resolve strengthened. She would use her voice to fight for change, to advocate for better protection for vulnerable children, to ensure that no more precious lives were lost to abuse and neglect. Jewel's memory would live on, not just in a song, but in

● ● ●

every life Maria's newfound voice could touch and potentially save. Her voice, once a silent whisper, would now join the chorus, a rising crescendo in the symphony of those speaking out against the darkness, demanding justice and protection for the innocent.

I touched the bunny charm at my throat, feeling its weight - the weight of memory, of promise, of hope. And I knew, with a certainty that resonated through my newly found voice, that this was just the beginning. The Silent Symphony would play on, and I would ensure that every note, every voice, was heard.

● ● ●